SIMON & SCHUSTER BOOKS FOR YOUNG READERS
Published by Simon & Schuster
New York • London • Toronto • Sydney • Tokyo • Singapore

Something's
Fishy

by John Schindel
illustrated by Maryann Cocca-Leffler

SIMON & SCHUSTER BOOKS FOR YOUNG READERS
Simon & Schuster Building, Rockefeller Center
1230 Avenue of the Americas, New York, New York 10020
Text copyright © 1993 by John Schindel
Illustrations copyright © 1993 Maryann Cocca-Leffler
SIMON & SCHUSTER BOOKS FOR YOUNG READERS
is a trademark of Simon & Schuster.
Designed by Vicki Kalajian
The text of this book was set in 18 pt. ITC Garamond Light.
The display type is Berliner Grotesk.
The illustrations were done in gouache and colored pencil.
Manufactured in the United States of America

10 9 8 7 6 5 4 3 2 1

Library of Congress Cataloging-in-Publication Data
Schindel, John. Something's fishy / John Schindel ; illustrated by Maryann Cocca-Leffler.
Summary: Roy visits a fishing hole harboring an octopus named Gus,
but what he pulls out on his fishing line is something of a surprise.
[1. Fishing—Fiction.   2. Octopus—Fiction.]   I. Cocca-Leffler, Maryann, ill.
II. Title.   PZ7.S346328So   1992   [E]—dc20   91-19223   CIP   ISBN 0-671-74777-0

For Pete DeFranco
—JS

To the three guppies,
Kristin, Connor & Cameron
—MCL

My Mom is the
best Mom

Roy was going fishing. He had his fishing pole and a basket of food.

Here is Roy's favorite fishing hole.
A big octopus named Gus lives somewhere
down there.

Roy lowered his line into the water and
waited.

Roy hooked something big! He reeled in his line faster and faster, and he pulled and he pulled. But it wasn't Gus at the end of the line. Roy pulled and up came a table.

Roy set the table under a tree. Then he lowered his line into the water and waited.

Roy hooked something again! He reeled
in his line, and he pulled and he pulled. This
time he pulled up two chairs.

Roy set the chairs next to the table. Then he
lowered his line into the water and waited.

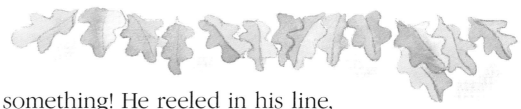

Roy had something! He reeled in his line, and he pulled. But it still wasn't Gus. Two plates popped out of the water.

Roy set a plate on the table in front of each chair. Then he lowered his line into the water and waited.

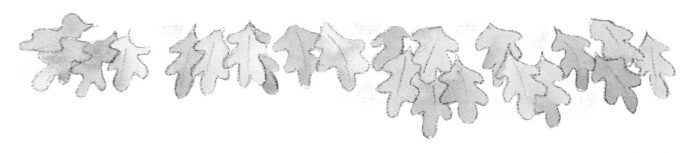

Another nibble! Roy reeled in his line.
Up came two cups.
　Roy set a cup in front of each plate.
Then he lowered his line one more time
and waited.

Something flashed in the water! Roy reeled in his line faster and faster, and he pulled and he pulled. Up came two knives, two forks, and two spoons.

Roy set one of each by the plates on the table. Then he opened his basket and laid out his food.

Fishing made Roy hungry.
Roy lowered himself onto his chair.

"Time for lunch, Gus," called Roy.

Gus pulled himself out of
the water and slithered
onto his chair.

"What's in your bag?"
asked Roy.

"One napkin for you," said Gus,
"and one napkin for me."

good

Book

My

MoM